George S. Boulger, Jean A. Owen

The Country Month by Month

Volume 1

George S. Boulger, Jean A. Owen

The Country Month by Month
Volume 1

ISBN/EAN: 9783337227128

Printed in Europe, USA, Canada, Australia, Japan

Cover: Foto ©Andreas Hilbeck / pixelio.de

More available books at **www.hansebooks.com**

The Country

Month by Month

BY

J. A. OWEN,

AUTHOR OF "FOREST, FIELD, AND FELL;"
AND EDITOR OF "A SON OF THE MARSHES;"

AND

Professor G. S. BOULGER, F.L.S., F.G.S.,

AUTHOR OF
"FAMILIAR TREES;" "THE USES OF PLANTS;" ETC.

COVER DESIGN BY J. LOCKWOOD KIPLING.

LONDON:

BLISS, SANDS AND FOSTER,

CRAVEN STREET, STRAND.

1894.

PREFACE.

IN the little monthly books, of which this is the first, we do not pretend to fine writing or essentially picturesque description. Our object is to try to direct the observation of lovers of Nature, busy dwellers in towns more especially, by telling them of some of the sights—we cannot, of course, in our small space enumerate all— that they may expect to find in their country wanderings month by month. If we are able to do this in any satisfactory measure we shall be glad.

THE AUTHORS.

CONTENTS.

———

The Country Month by Month.

MARCH.

A S we can still gather from the numerical names of the last four months in our calendar, the ancient Roman year began with March, and there is much to be said in favour of this old arrangement. In towns or suburbs we may only have noticed that the rains of February have washed some of the soot from the bark of our trees, and that, now all continuous frost is over, the ground is soft and moist; but in the country there is a general feeling of renewed life. It is not that a few evergreens or brightly-coloured fruits console us with the thought that as winter was preceded by summer so also will summer come again: it is not that the chill-looking snowdrops, those "fair maids of February," peep through snow or dead leaves; but, as Miss Rossetti says—

"Life's alive in everything."

The boughs still look bare as they sway in the brisk wind; but this very swaying may assist in pumping up the sap in the stem; and the buds, though still covered with their brown winter scales, are swelling to the bursting. March winds may be keen; but they seem to make the blood flow more swiftly in our veins. We no longer feel the dank mists of November presaging the nipping hopelessness of winter: we are surrounded by hope; and at our feet, if not so obviously above our heads, there is already a wealth of greenness and even of flower, if we will but look for it, a wealth undreamt of by many "in populous city pent." The fox-hunter knows the woodlands in March, and only the most bigoted of his kind will blame the violets for spoiling the scent. The permanent resident in the country cannot fail to see many an early blossom by the roadside, whilst the cottage garden soon becomes gay with flowers; but the townsman knows little or nothing of the country in March. He may have visited it amid the snows of Christmas; but he rarely thinks of a country ramble before Easter as presenting any possibilities of enjoyment. Let us tempt the dweller in the country to wander yet further afield, and the citizen

> "Here in this roaring moon of daffodil
> And crocus, to put forth and brave the blast."

As we start we may speculate as to whether the ancients, in dedicating this month to Mars, that somewhat blustering god, had any thought of the appropriateness of their act from the meteorological point of view; or as to who would be the purchaser of this cloud of March dust, if we were to gather it, at the market rate of a guinea a peck or a king's ransom per bushel. Let us go then to

> "... feel the bluff North blow again
> And mark the sprouting thistle
> Set up on waste patch of the lane
> Its green and tender bristle,
> And spy the scarce-blown violet-banks,
> Crisp primrose-leaves and others,
> And watch the lambs leap at their pranks,
> And butt their patient mothers."

THE PLANT-WORLD IN MARCH.

BY BANK AND COPSE.

" Young leaves clothe early hedgerow trees ;
Seeds, and roots, and stones of fruits,
Swollen with sap, put forth their shoots ;
Curled-headed ferns sprout in the lane ;
Birds sing and pair again."—CHRISTINA ROSSETTI.

THE March sun has not much strength ; so that we are not likely to find many flowers as yet in the denser thickets of a wood, or on any bank facing the north. By the sunny roadside hedgerow, or among the open coppice not long felled, we shall find the greatest number of the flowers of March. Whether our ramble be in the Midland or the South-Eastern counties, or in the earlier Norfolk or South-West, or in the later North of higher ground in Wales, will make a difference of from one to three weeks in the dates of Nature's year, on either side of what we may term the Midland and South-Eastern average. So too, if we repeat our ramble over the same ground after an interval of two or three weeks, we shall find a marked advance. What was then in bursting bud is now in leaf: what was in leaf may now be in flower: flowers, then few, now abound: flowers, then fully out, are now fading to their disappearance. If then "the season's difference," or the early date of our visit, disappoint us of some beauty which we were led to expect, it will often only be necessary for us to go again, and, so going, we may rest assured that, if we use our eyes and ears, many another beauty, though unexpected, will be ours.

At the outset of our walk perhaps we come to a roadside farm with apple-orchard and old-fashioned garden. Here on some veteran tree, of no great value for its fruit, hangs a reminder of Christmas, a bunch of mistletoe conspicuous midst the bare grey crooked apple-boughs in its vivid yellow-green. It is now in flower; but its insignificant greenish blossoms, though presenting some points of interest to the botanist, are less familiar than its pearly berries. If the bunch happen to be a male one (for in this species the sexes are on different plants) the little four-cleft flowers will well repay examination, for each segment bears on its surface a honeycomb-like stamen, which discharges its pollen in this unusual way through many openings. As the bough hangs, growing, unlike most plants, mainly in a downward direction, one is reminded that from this fact, according to the quaint old-world medical doctrine of signatures, mistletoe was looked upon as a specific for giddiness or epilepsy, the "falling sickness" of our ancestors.

From the short grass beneath the apple-trees spreads a wide patch of the glossy green frills of the winter aconite; but its golden stars of blossom have nearly all been washed away by the rain. Close by rise in the stiffness of their youth the narrow grey-green leaves of a tuft of daffodils, among which a few flower-stalks bear pointed yellow-tinged buds, already swollen beyond the restraint of the shrivelling membranous sheath that enclosed them. Their plumpness suggests, or perhaps one or two just-opened flowers may reveal, that these are the double garden variety. Its blossoms exhibit an endless succession of closely-packed strips of alternating yellow and orange, the one with cut edge, the other simply pointed, representing respectively the leaves of the perianth and the tubular coronet, indefinitely repeated by that splitting process which French botanists well term *dédoublement.*

The garden in front of the house, though with ridged rows of celery, many lanky Brussels sprouts, and much else of a strictly utilitarian character, yet is bright with many a homely flower, recalling Perdita's catalogue in the *Winter's Tale—*

> " Daffodils,
> That come before the swallow dares, and take
> The winds of March with beauty ; violets dim,
> But sweeter than the lids of Juno's eyes,
> Or Cytherea's breath ; pale primroses,
> That die unmarried, ere they can behold
> Bright Phœbus in his strength ; bold oxlips, and
> The crown imperial ; lilies of all kinds."

The straight gravel walk has perhaps an edging of double crimson daisies, and the border, narrowed by the demand for vegetables, may yet be gay with scarlet or purple anemones with their black centres, or with clumps of crocuses, golden, purple, and white. Even an early Van Thol tulip may blaze among its sober grey-green foliage, and the rosy clusters may hang from amid the young green fans of the Ribes leaves. Though this so-called " flowering currant," introduced from North America within the present century, has become familiar in the garden even of the cottager, and is recognised as a currant even by children, the Latin name common to the whole group still clings more particularly to it, as does Trifolium to the crimson clover. Close by, its humbler, but more useful kinsfolk, the red currant and the gooseberry, droop their greenish clusters from twigs whose opening buds breathe the first scent of spring, now, however, eclipsed in fragrance by the "leafless pink mezereons" beside them. We shall indeed be fortunate if, when our early spring rambles take us into some wood on a limestone soil, we light upon this rarest of our native shrubs, humble in its growth, bare as yet of leaves, but "thick beset with blushing wreaths" of the sweetest pink tubular flowerets. If we try to gather it without a knife the toughness of its flexible shoots will remind us of its kinship to the lace-barks of the tropics, which furnish stout bast for the rope-maker.

If the owner love the old-fashioned favourites of our fathers, the curious hen-and-chickens daisy may be here, with early polyanthus and the grape- and cluster-hyacinths. From beneath the main head of minute florets, the outer ones strap-shaped and white or pink-tipped, the inner ones tubular and yellow, which the botanist with his pocket lens will show us constitutes a daisy, peep several little stalks, each bearing a daisy in miniature, suggesting newly-hatched nestlings just leaving the wing of the brooding hen. A little searching in our woodlands in spring will reveal primroses that are not only the pale yellow hue that suggests to our poets nothing but thoughts of unloved sorrow, but of almost every shade from purest white to pink and even bright red. Many of these may also vary in having a long common stalk to their flowers, like the cowslip ; and, if transplanted in November, will originate fresh stocks of polyanthuses in our gardens, as no doubt the first of their varied kind originated. These quaintly stiff little plants, with numerous little globular blue flowers clustered together at the upper end of a glossy green stalk, are the starch- or cluster- and grape-hyacinths, and, though often not in flower till May, and not truly wild, may sometimes be met with in situations where they have probably escaped from cultivation.

The fragrant charms of the mezereon, and the gold and purple glories of the crocuses, are, after all, but very transient, whilst the crown imperial has in the March flower-bed a dignity all its own. Its stout stems, with their bright, luxuriant leaves, rise two feet or more from the bulb; and, though its tulip-like blossoms of pale lemon-yellow or deep brownish-red do hang downwards, their number and size seem fully to justify its name. A native of Persia, Afghanistan, and Cashmere, we shall find its more lowly congener the fritillary, as a wilding in our meadows a little later in the year. Chapman, a contemporary of Shakespere, calls it—

"Fair crown imperial, emperor of flowers ; "

and John Parkinson, but a few years later, in his *Paradisus Terrestris*, says that it "for its stately beautifulnesse deserveth the first place in this our garden of delight, to be entreated of before all other Lillies." Most of the varieties we have now, some of which have leaves striped with white or yellow, existed in his time. But let us look a little more closely at the flower itself, and if we lift one of the blossoms what we see within cannot be better described than it was by Gerard in 1597. "In the bottome of each of the bells," he says, "there is placed six drops of most cleere shining sweet water, in taste like sugar, resembling in shew faire Orient pearles, the which drops if you take away there do immediately appeare the like; notwithstanding, if they be suffered to stand still in the floure according to his owne nature, they wil never fall away, no, not if you strike the plant untill it be broken." It is probable that in the native country of this interesting plant these drops of nectar, secreted in conspicuous white hollows at the bases of the perianth-leaves, serve to attract insects which are useful in transporting the pollen to another flower. The interesting observation has, however, been made that these nectariferous glands, as also those of the grass of Parnassus, and of the Christmas roses and other hellebores, have a power of absorbing nitrogenous food, their cells undergoing a characteristic internal change on their doing so. It has therefore been suggested that the glands are insectivorous organs; but this is improbable in the case of a floral structure, flowers being concerned with seed-production rather than with feeding; and it may be suggested that the delicate walls of the cells of such glands, though normally excretive, are capable under abnormal conditions of what may be called reversal of function. Leaving scientific questions, however, we may recall a pretty German legend, which tells us that these flowers were originally erect and white; but that when our Lord passed through the garden of Gethsemane on the night of the agony, and all the other flowers bent in sorrowing worship, they alone remained unmoved until sorrow and shame overcame pride, and they have ever since had bending heads, blushing faces, and flowing tears.

But we must not linger longer, even among the fascinations of a rustic garden; for we are in search of the

beauties of wild Nature this morning. The garden flowers
of spring are too precious, or too beautiful as they grow,
for us to gather them, and their owner moreover is absent.
He has much to engage his attention just at present.
Passing through his plough land, where perchance there
is already the first gleaming shimmer of young wheat in
the fitful sunlight, we may find him sowing oats, or,
mindful of the adage—

> "David and Chad,
> Sow peas, good or bad :
> If they're not in by Benedick,
> They had better stop in the rick,"

hastening, whatever the weather, to get both peas and
beans into the ground between the first two days and the
twenty-first of the month. He may be rolling his grass,
planting a few willow cuttings as a fence round his pond,
or setting quick along some new hedge-row.

We have not far to go along this lane before we come to
a wild plant in flower. True, it is but a weed, its blossoms
are of the smallest, they are white, and you may find them
almost anywhere during nine months out of the twelve, yet
it is not without interest. It is the little "shepherd's-purse,"
as it is called in most European languages, the "pick-
purse," "pick-pocket," "mother's heart," or, more tragically,
"pick your mother's heart out," of some of our country
children. Here it is growing under a wall in the dust of
the footpath, its tuft of jagged root-leaves already be-
smirched with the first dust of the year. Some of the
little cruciform flowers are already over, and, as the main
flower-stalk has lengthened, carrying up its close, flat
terminal cluster of buds, these first flowers are represented
by the heart-shaped pods to which the plant owes most of

its names. A mediæval shepherd may have carried a leathern pouch of this form, and he would have been fortunate if it held as many pence as this pod does seeds. The plant is now looked upon merely as a prolific weed ; but formerly it was supposed to have many merits, and "poor man's parmacetie" was among its numerous names. Wild throughout the North of the Old World, it has followed civilization into every temperate region, and presents several varieties which the botanical student may do well to study for practice in nice discrimination. One of them has no petals, but ten stamens, instead of the normal six.

As our gaze is directed at this bit of wall, a more minute flowering plant attracts our attention, as it springs from among the velvety cushions of moss in the crevices whence the mortar has long perished. Here on the top of the wall it grows, the spring whitlow-grass. For its description we will once more refer to John Gerard, "Master in Chirurgerie" of three hundred years ago. "It is," he says, "a very slender plant, having a few small leaves like the least chick-weede, growing in little tufts, from the midst whereof rises up a small stalk, nine inches long, on whose top do growe verie little white flowers; which being past, there come in place small, flat pouches, composed of three films ; which being ripe, the two outsides fall away, leaving the middle part standing long time after, which is like white satin." Its stalk is less often nine inches high than two or three ; but otherwise this account is strikingly graphic. The plant is very acrid, as are so many of the mustard and cress family, to which it and the shepherd's-purse alike belong, and this acridity was formerly believed to be good for that painful disease of the nail known as a whitlow, to which the plant was applied with milk. For this reason it was also sometimes called "nail-wort," nearly all our plants which have popular names ending in "wort" being old herbalist's remedies. The little plant varies very much, in the shape of its satiny pods and in other minor points; so that a French botanist has actually described no less than seventy forms, which he finds remain distinct when cultivated.

Growing with this tiny fairy-like plant on the wall, or spreading perhaps with it to the adjoining bank, we may find, though not yet in flower, another curious little annual, the three-fingered saxifrage, a reddish plant, but a few inches high, with three-fingered leaves, sticky, as is the whole plant, with minute red-knobbed hairs, adhering to which we may even already discover some unfortunate small insects.

A suggestion of green is now seen all along the hedge-rows. Both quick-set and blackthorn are still bare; but here and there the stout, brown, warty shoots of the elder are putting out tufts of leaves: the wild briars are already well clothed with their delicate and vivid foliage; and in places we may perhaps see one of the guelder-roses un-folding its pleated leaves. A gust of the keen spring air is driving before it the bright white clouds: the sun bursts out momentarily with unwonted power, and we see flying gaily before us, with its characteristic zigzag flight, a brilliant vision of life, of resurrection. It settles for a moment on the bank, and as it closes its sulphur wings it reveals the beautiful curves of their angular outlines. It is the Brim-stone butterfly; but, though its caterpillar fed on some buckthorn bush not far from here, this lovely insect left its green chrysalis late last autumn, and after flying about for a day or two, passed into that winter sleep from which to-day's sunshine has awakened it. If this sunshine continues, its warmth intensified towards the afternoon, we may meet several other kinds of butterflies; but all of them at this season will probably be similarly hibernated specimens. Since the wonderful invasion of a few years back, we may even live in hopes of viewing upon the wing that grand insect the Camberwell Beauty, with white-bordered, claret-coloured wings stretching three inches and a half, which it is so difficult for us to associate with the trim villadom of Camberwell, though it was caught there less than fifty years ago. Probably every schoolboy who ever started a collection has anxiously scanned many an old and ragged small tortoise-shell in the hopes of capturing a Comma; and does familiarity ever breed contempt of such beautiful objects as a Painted Lady or a Red Admiral? The butterflies of the tropics may be larger and more lustrous with metallic sheen; but they cannot surpass the delicacy of colouring of the under surface of the one, or the rich velvet tints of the other, of these British insects. Their names are homely, but their tints seem suggestive of some palace in fairyland.

The sight of the bright spot of yellow fluff disporting in the sunshine has for the moment set us thinking that the wild flowers we have come across in our walk have as yet been merely white. True, we have only gone a few yards and here is another little white blossom in the bank beside us. No, it is not a strawberry. It is the humble poor relation of the strawberry, known generally as the barren strawberry. Its little leaves are not unlike those of its more sought-after relative, but more silky, with fine hairs, and so less self-assertive. Its blossoms too are very

strawberry-like, though smaller and with notched petals;
but it may be at once distinguished at this season by its
slender, drooping stalk, which seems to say, "My fruit will
be small, dry, and uninteresting to you, not the richly-
flavoured berry of my proud and stiff-stalked cousin."
Here, at last, however, the sunshine seems to have
awakened some sympathetic brightness in the plant-world,
for the whole hedgerow before us is a sparkling blaze with
the many-pointed rays of the lesser celandine—Wordsworth's lesser celandine—shining among its own glossy
leaves. There are plenty of green unopened buds among
these burnished golden stars, however; but some of the
blossoms bear unmistakable signs of February's rains.
We might have gathered them a month ago; now they are
bleached to a whitish pallor that makes their gold seem as
dross.

We dart forward with a shout of joy to the first violets
of spring. Is not the bank covered with them, standing
before us in unusual prominence and size? Alas! no.
We have been so deceived before, and may often be so
again. The wish was father to the thought, and we may
very probably detect the modest violet presently by its
perfume before it discloses itself to our eyes; but this is
only ground-ivy. Only ground-ivy! And yet, though
common enough, and with a perfume rather unpleasant
than fragrant, it is a pretty little plant, and a plant with a
history. It is not much like an ivy; and, though its
leaves are rounded and softly downy, their many indenta-
tions are not very suggestive of a cat's-foot, though cat's-
foot is one of its many popular names. Its deep violet
flowers are in groups of three in the angle between each
leaf and the reddish prostrate stem; and, when we come

to look at them at closer quarters, are not the least violet-like in form.   They are little trumpet-shaped tubes with two lobes on one side of their mouths and three spread out on the other.   "Blue-runner," "Robin run in the hedge," or "Gill go by the ground," are names the application of which is obvious ; but some explanation is perhaps necessary of the fact of so humble a plant having so many popular appellations, and this explanation we get in the two additional names "Ale-hoof" and "Tun-foot." This now despised plant was the predecessor of the hop in Old English brewing, having an aromatic bitter taste ; and the leaves were compared by our ancestors to a foot or hoof, as were those of dozens of other plants.

If the season be an early one we may hope to find either the field scorpion-grass, or more probably the yet earlier species, the scientific name of which *(collina)* implies inaccurately that it is specially characteristic of hills.   Both these dry land representatives of the more attractive forget-me-not have minute blue flowers, only an eighth or a sixth of an inch across; but perhaps the most obvious distinctions between them are that the former (the field species) has its leaves stalked and each flower furnished with a stalk several times longer than itself, whilst the early species has hardly any stalk to the leaves, the separate flower-stalks not longer than the flowers themselves, and (most easily recognised of characters) one little flower some distance below the rest.   Whilst the Latin name of the genus *(Myosotis)*, meaning "mouse-ear," applies to their downy leaves, the old English name, "scorpion-grass," refers probably to the way in which the stalk of flowers is rolled up in the bud, suggesting the tail of a scorpion. This, as also the surface rough with hairs, is, however, characteristic of almost all the borage family, to which these plants belong.

A patch of waste land or common here separates us from yonder wood. A hobbled donkey is searching vainly for young shoots round a close-grazed furze-bush, and a few geese are paddling round the sides of a small and dirty pond. The soil hereabouts is stiff. An old and straggling bush of "the never bloomless furze," tangled with a hawthorn above the reach of the donkey, bears a few of its golden blossoms. Norse folk-lore is credited with terming March "the lengthening month that wakes the adder and blooms the whin"; and, though we might in the South find a few flowers on the furze in February, in the North, where more particularly it is called whin, the saying is undoubtedly true. On an exceptionally warm day we may perhaps find an adder sunning himself on some such spot as this; but he is likely to be still but half emerged from his winter torpor. This large-growing furze, and the dwarf allied forms between them, keep up that constant succession of blossom that leads to the adage that "kissing is out of season when the furze is out of blossom"; but the dwarf species are more common on sand, while this larger one loves the clay. We cannot resist, in this season when floral perfumes are still scarce, gathering a few of the bright blossoms with their soft, woolly, two-lipped coats, to rub them in our hands, and sniff their rich apricot-like fragrance. As we step aside to do so we light upon a whole assemblage of weedy plants that have evidently been some time in bloom. Here the deep pink gaping flowers of the red dead-nettle peep out between its crowded red-tinged leaves: the despised groundsel, a degraded Cineraria without the bright ray-florets of its relatives, is growing side by side with some chickweed, alike patronised by the keepers of pet birds; and perhaps an early dandelion is eclipsing the brightness of a group of leafless coltsfoot. We may note the deeply-notched white petals of the chickweed, each looking like two, and the single row of minute hairs along its stem, which curiously shifts its position from one side of the stem to the other at every pair of leaves. The dandelion springs from a rosette of the deeply-toothed leaves to which it owes its name, its smooth and hollow milky stalk surmounted with recurved green bracts or scales below the head of strap-shaped florets. The coltsfoot on the other hand, like many another flower of spring, produces its flowers in advance of the leaves, and thus is now seen only as a flower-stalk, woolly, and bearing numerous small leafy scales, surmounted by its paler yellow, thistle-like head of florets, of which only the outer ones are long and narrow.

From the gold at our feet we look up to gold over our heads. Here the hedgerow has become the rendezvous for quite a crowd of busily humming bees, the first we have noticed abroad this year; for here a large sallow is in all the glory of its golden palm. So too, we now notice, are a group of little prostrate forms, with trailing wiry stems of glossy brown, in the swampy ground near the pond. The low-growing shrub is the hedgerow-tree in miniature. They have burst their brown bud-scales, and the oval cushion of silver fur now appears thickly studded with the gold-headed threads, among which the bees are so hard at work. The legs of the insects are so laden with the golden pollen that they seem hardly able to fly; yet if we watch them we may trace some of them to another tree yonder, which at once strikes us as different. Instead of the plump, oval, gold-studded balls, each with something of an upward growth, it bears longer catkins, with a more horizontal direction, and clad in more sober silver-grey without a particle of gold. These are the "silver pussy palms" of the children, and it is they only that will bear fruit in summer, when the golden palms of the other tree have faded into nothingness; for the former are collections of flowers, each consisting of a downy ovary with a sticky stigma, to which the bees or the wind carry the fertilising pollen from the other trees. Yonder "hedgerow elm" and the hazels we can see from here at the edge of the wood, alike illustrate this production of flowers before the leaves in the windy season. The boughs of the elm waving in their lace-like tracery against the sky catch a rich claret hue in the fleeting sunlight. This is from their clusters of flowers, which have red anthers, as those of the willow have golden ones; but in this case pollen-bearing anthers and stigma-bearing ovary are in the same little flower, and perhaps it only requires a little March breeze to shake the pollen from the one on to the sticky surface of the other.

To reach the wood there is yet a field for us to cross. A gate stands open for a horse-drill that is working in one part of the field, and as we pass it we are greeted with the wished-for perfume. Now it is violets in earnest, the sweet violets of the end of March, that may be found as early as the middle of February, but too often are not out before the equinox—here they are, purple and white ones growing together in the grass of this hedge-row bank, so fragrant and so beautiful that we expect to be called profane if we do not abandon ourselves to simple admiration. But knowledge, and not ignorance, is the true parent of reverential wonder. Our appreciation of the beauty of a flower is heightened and not lessened by the knowledge that each curve in its outline, and each spot of colour on its petal has a definite utility in the plant economy. We love violets; but we do not for that reason refrain from studying them. The green leaves of the calyx are parted to make room for the spur of the corolla, and the petals are marked with finely-ruled lines leading to the mouth of this spur. Each of the five stamens splits in two lines down its inner surface to discharge its pollen, and each is furnished with a curious little rusty-brown triangular tip. Two out of the five have also tail-like appendages which extend backwards into the spur, and secrete the honey with which it is filled; and finally above the ovary rises a curious hooded style, like a bird's head, with a hole at the side, in which is the stigma. Judging by other plants we should say that we have in the violet an elaborate series of contrivances for what botanists call insect cross-pollination, *i.e.*, the conveyance of pollen by insect agency from one flower to another. Here is the pollen: here is the attractive scent: here is the rewarding honey and the "honey-guides," as the fine lines are termed, to lead the insect visitor; but the insect visitor hardly ever comes, and it is not these elaborately-contrived flowers that produce the large crop of seed on our violet-beds in autumn. Later in the season, on shorter stalks, inconspicuous bud-like flowers will appear, but will not open. They will have neither perfume nor honey, nor will any insect enter them; but they it is that bear the well-filled seed-capsules of autumn. The production of these "cleistogene" flowers, as they are termed, is still one of the puzzles of the biologist. Nature seems to have altered her mind. The elaborately contrived and perfumed flower may fulfil its appointed end by securing an occasional cross, or it may have become a failure from the scarcity of insect life in early March; but the fact remains that it is the violets, rather than the primroses, "that die unmarried," as Shakespeare puts it.

I can already see primroses beneath the coppice in the wood across the field, so we will hasten over the ploughed land as best we may to reach them; but spring flowers are too few for us to pass them by, and here at our feet, in the furrows that have stood fallow during the winter, is a dainty little creeping plant, with pale blue blossoms, that seem to reflect the spring-tide heavens. It is the ivy-leaved speedwell, the first of its race to greet the year, though it will continue to flower till midsummer. Its rather fleshy pale-green leaves have five or seven lobes, and are thus not unlike the ivy. The entirely blue colour of its little flowers —they are but the sixth of an inch across—distinguishes it from some of its near allies; and you may already find perhaps one of its distinctly two-lobed capsules.

We have reached the ditch surrounding the wood, over which hang the hazel-bushes we saw from the other side of the field. It is not so choked with vegetation as it will be a few months hence. Some "leaf-nested primroses" are ensconced under the gnarled roots of the hazels, but they are out of our reach as yet. The carpet of dog's mercury, with its vivid green, is neither so thick nor so deep as it will be; but many plants from it too have found their way through the hedge, and we can see a variety of budding flowers among it. We must, however, just stop to gather and examine a catkin from these hazel-bushes. It is swaying in the breeze, and sending out clouds of golden dust. It hangs down fully two inches in length, slightly tapering, and no doubt suggesting a little cat's tail, the origin of our word "catkin."

The books tell us that a catkin is a deciduous spike; but let us see for ourselves. If we take one of these fully-developed examples, and not those dull brown sausage-like buds at the end of yonder bough, we see it has a number of little scales, and under each of these a pocket lens will show us two smaller ones or "bracteoles," each with two forked stamens between it and the central stalk. Thus, as each stamen bifurcates, every catkin-scale or "bract" covers eight of the anthers that are now so busily discharging their pollen. This structure is explained by comparison with other catkins as representing two flowers below each bract, a central one being undeveloped; so that the entire catkin is more complex in its structure than a spike, in which the flowers are typically arranged in a single linear, or rather spiral, series. When the wind has blown all their pollen away these catkins will have exchanged their present almost primrose hue for one decidedly greener; but what will have become of the pollen? There are no leaves on the trees to obstruct it, and that which is to come to anything must probably go to another tree. It is true that here, on the upper side of this same branch, are several of the little egg-shaped female catkins, with their few overlapping scales topped with clustering crimson points; but these stigmas are not yet sticky, so that pollen will not adhere to them.

We can wait no longer, but are busily filling our baskets with primroses. Their crinkled leaves are still small, and all their stalks blush with the pink of youth. The "rathe," or early primrose of Milton, is short moreover in the stalk; but in the bunch their perfume is as delicate as it will ever be, and dotted about here and there in the open coppice they are perhaps more picturesque than when carpeting an entire bank. Only perhaps in inner recesses of the wood shall we find the drawn-up specimens with several flowers borne aloft on a single stalk, which most country folk erroneously know as "oxlips," and which serve to explain the apparent difference in the arrangement of the flowers in primrose and in cowslip. Each primrose flower has, it is true, a long and slender stalk, far longer than is the case in the cowslip, and these stalks rise deep down among the bases of the leaves; but there we shall find them united on a common stalk, as are those of the cowslip, only that here the conditions are reversed, and this "peduncle," or footstalk, as it is termed, is long in the cowslip, and, as a rule, extremely short in the primrose.

We have gathered a large bunch, picking at the same time a few of the delicate drooping wood-anemones, blushing pink over the contrasting dark green of the three cut leaves that spring from the middle of their flower-stalks. As we have been so engaged we have seen that the dog's-mercury is in flower; that there is many a patch of lesser celandine, and perhaps the little verdigris oil-beetle feeding on its leaves; that the firm and polished green spears of the wild hyacinths are piercing their way up through the dead leaves, often carrying aloft in triumph a withered transfixed victim; but that they have not yet reached the flowering stage. Several other plants also we may have noticed. The stout crimson stalks and blue-green leaves of the wood-spurge, now hanging drooping heads, are conspicuous, though less so perhaps than they

will be when they rise erect to flower.   Here and there a
pointed glossy-green shoot, well wrapped round with its
leaves, marks the coming of the cuckoo-pint, or lords-and-
ladies, next month; and perhaps a spreading rosette of
polished leaves, irregularly blotched snake-like with
purplish red, may similarly herald the early purple orchis.
From tawny heaps of decaying leaves the curled fronds of
ferns are beginning to show themselves, and we find in this
and other respects considerable difference between the
open coppice where we are standing, which was felled in
the autumn before last, and the denser thickets where the
spring sun has not yet made itself felt.

Here, however, at our feet, is an interesting little plant
which we were nearly overlooking, among dog's-mercury
and wood-anemones. Its little leaves resemble in form those
of the latter, but are of a brighter and lighter green.   Its
flower-stalk bears two leafy bracts, like the three in the
anemone, and its little head of green flowers at first sight
looks like the fruit of the anemone when the flowers have
fallen.   It is the moschatel, musk crowfoot, musk-root,
hollow root, or bulbous fumitory, so called from its musky
odour, which is strongest at evening, and its thick white
hollow underground stem.   It is difficult to think of it as
the near ally of the elder and the honeysuckle; but its
little flowers are well worth looking at.   There are five of
them, forming five sides of a cube of which the stalk
occupies the base: the upper flower has four little green
petals and eight stamens, and the four side ones have each
five petals and five deeply two-forked stamens, the whole
forming a cube hardly half an inch in diameter.   Close to
it is growing the hairy wood-rush, which differs from the
true rushes in having flat, grass-like leaves, and grows

nearly a foot high, its slender stem bearing long, scattered hairs, and each branch ending in a solitary chestnut-brown, rush-like flower. Rushes seem indeed to be but fallen representatives of the grand lily tribe; but by a happy accident we light hard by upon two far less common and nearer representatives of that group. This little yellow star-of-Bethlehem is decidedly lily-like. It has a little bulb (though the plant is so rare I should be sorry to pull it up to demonstrate the fact), one long narrow sheathing hyacinth-like leaf and a little umbel of six-rayed greenish-yellow stars. These greenish-yellow flower-leaves are, it has been suggested, an ancient survival, the ancestral type of how the first petals arose from altered yellow stamens. But if this little plant be a lily, what shall we say to this sturdy prickly little shrub? My friends will hardly believe me when I say that this butcher's-broom too is a lily. Yet so it is. Its tough green stems, the only woody ones among British members, not only of the lily family, but of the great class of which that family is but a small part, are simply palm stems in little, and afford interesting proof of this under the microscope. Butchers still use it as a broom in some country towns; and in the New Forest, where it is plentiful, it is known as knee-holm or knee-holly from its height, its evergreen character, and its prickly points. The little greenish flowers you see are in the centre of the broad flat pointed leaf-like structure, though botanists tell us that flowers never grow on leaves; but those are not the leaves: they are the minute scales you see below each of these leaf-like branches. Here one of last winter's scarlet berries remains, like that of the lily of the valley or the asparagus, and this last-mentioned plant is indeed one of the nearest allies of the butcher's-broom.

Let us hasten on. A companion who knows the locality has yet a treat in store. We push our way under the ghostly dead-seeming boughs of some young larches, and come out at the head of a slope facing south, a different side of the wood from that on which we entered, and there before us waves a sea of glorious daffodils. I know few, if any, keener pleasure in store for the lover of wild flowers, the whole year through. We may find many a rarer plant than the Lent lily, as it is often called,—the yellow star-of-Bethlehem, for instance, is far less common;—but there is but little comparison between the joyous glee with which this sight fills one, and the merely intellectual pleasure of a "rare find." Wordsworth's poem rises to our lips, for this is the time for poetry and not for science; and, familiar as it is, we make no excuse for quoting it in full. It is the verses of Wordsworth, the lover of nature, that endear themselves to us rather than the courtly conceits of Herrick, who could walk through the lovely Devonshire lanes round his home at Dean Prior, lanes draped in ferns and primroses, and complain of "this dull Devonshire."

> " I wander'd lonely as a cloud
>   That floats on high o'er vales and hills,
> When all at once I saw a crowd,
>   A host of golden daffodils,
> Beside the lake beneath the trees
> Fluttering and dancing in the breeze.
>
> " Continuous as the stars that shine
>   And twinkle on the milky-way,
> They stretched in never-ending line
>   Along the margin of a bay :
> Ten thousand saw I at a glance,
> Tossing their heads in sprightly dance.

" The waves beside them danced, but they
   Out-did the sparkling waves in glee :—
A poet could not but be gay
   In such a jocund company !
I gazed—and gazed—but little thought
What wealth the show to me had brought ;

" For oft, when on my couch I lie
   In vacant or in pensive mood,
They flash upon that inward eye
   Which is the bliss of solitude ;
And then my heart with pleasure fills,
And dances with the daffodils."

We recall too that it was of daffodils that Keats wrote
the now too hackneyed line, " A thing of beauty is a joy
for ever "; and the deliberate utterance of Mahomet, " He
that has two cakes of bread, let him sell one of them for
some flower of the narcissus ; for bread is the food of the
body ; but narcissus is food for the soul." Then, when
our emotional ardour has a little cooled, we may discuss
the many names of our favourite, such as " Lent rose,"
" crown bells," " chalice-flower," and " daffadowndilly,"
and whether this last be but a playful modification of
daffodil, or, as is credibly alleged, a corruption of saffron
lily. Then too the question arises whether this beautiful
flower is truly wild, and we note that its leaves have less
grey bloom upon them than those of the cultivated form ;
that the six floral leaves are of a paler yellow, and that the
lovely deep golden coronet in their centre has rectangular,
instead of rounded, lobings to its gracefully recurved
margin. Bulbous plants often spread far, and it is hard to
say where there may not have been a monastic garden or
the orchard of a mediæval grange ; but the daffodil would

never perhaps have been doubted to be a truly British
plant did not its very beauty suggest a sunnier clime as
the land of its birth.   Now, alas ! it is being ruthlessly
sacrificed to our smoky towns, not flowers only, but even
the roots.   Too truly,

> " Now fair Daffodilla is coming to town
> In a yellow petticoat and a green gown,"

and so perhaps must we, though less gaily bedecked.

IN THE RIVER MEADS.

> " In the wind of windy March
> The catkins drop down,
> Curly, caterpillar-like,
> Curious green and brown."—ROSSETTI.

THESE lines recur to my mind as, on a blustering day about the vernal equinox, I start on a short stroll through some water-meadows to a withy eyot close to the river bank. The yet leafless boughs of some tall aspens are waving to and fro overhead, and now and again a big wine-red catkin, which has not yet begun to shed its pollen, is torn off by the breeze and flung at my feet. The day is overcast, and at this season the entomologist thinks rather of hunting for larvæ under dead leaves than of capturing the perfect insect. A good deal may still be done by that judicious blending of green treacle and rum, mixed on the spot, that has superseded the "sugaring" of the last half-century. The March Dagger moth may now be met with on stems, and the Light Orange-underwing, the Early Grey, the Clouded Drab and the Hebrew-character moth, especially on willows. The dark grey stems of the alders in this swampy piece of ground seem to accord well with the dull sky, and can hardly be said to be relieved by the dull green of their short, globose catkins, which swing among the woody, cone-like remains of those of previous years. But here at their feet is a relief from the dull monotony of their colouring. We find we are standing on peat, veritable peat, which a walking-stick assures us is at least three feet in depth, but which is composed almost entirely, not of bog-moss, but of the tiny golden saxifrages, both species growing together, the one with its little bright green and fleshy round leaves in pairs, the other bearing them singly, and both with flat clusters of tiny golden flowers. I said "almost entirely," for there are scattered bunches of the far larger marsh-marigold, the "water-blobs" of our Surrey childhood, flaunting their sturdier growth, as if proud of the wealth of gold they are now beginning to display in their unfolding sepals. It is certainly a curious point in structural botany that these brilliantly metallic charms, so like the petals of the buttercup, should yet correspond in origin rather with the green external leaves of the latter flower, though both are nearly related in other points. Yellow is certainly the chief floral colour we shall meet with to-day; for here the willows are in bloom, especially the purple osier with its polished red-purple stems. These stems are almost as commonly used for basket-making as the more silky common osier, which will not be in flower for another month. Here comes the rain, however, and there seems but little prospect of variety at present among water-side plants, so we will abandon the quest.

ON A CHALK SUBSOIL.

NO right-thinking person will wish to do anything by word or deed that may lead to the extermination of any of our British plants, so we do not propose to describe in detail any visit to the homes of our chief rarities. We might go at this season to the lonely ruins of Pennard Castle in the peninsula of Gower, about eight miles from Swansea, where in almost inaccessible security grows the yellow Alpine whitlow-grass; whilst on neighbouring limestone cliffs we might light upon the somewhat less uncommon rock hutchinsia, a pretty little relative of the homely shepherd's-purse, with "pinnate" or feather-like divisions to its leaves. We will however go less far afield. There are at all seasons of the year a considerable number of interesting plants that, requiring a well-drained and warm subsoil, grow preferably upon limestone, or in the South-East of England on our prevalent earthy limestone, the chalk. We may go to the gloomy shade of the box-trees on Box-hill in Surrey, and no doubt we shall find thereabouts the scentless hairy violet growing in the open pastures; or we may visit the ever-beautiful slopes of Cliefden, where the aged yew-trees overshadow the luridly poisonous hellebores; but there is a special reason why we should choose some part of Essex, Suffolk, Cambridgeshire, or Hertfordshire, approximately between Bishop Stortford, Haverhill, Linton, and Saffron Walden. Here in the roadside ditches we shall see the fern-like foliage and perhaps the just-opening white umbels of the cow-parsley, which we were too preoccupied with other interests to notice in our previous ramble. Now too perhaps the wood violet, then only in bud, may be in flower, as also in shady spots the pale veined flowers of the wood-sorrel amid its first delicate pink - stalked and silky leaves. Yes, it is to the woods we must go, and there we shall find, perhaps with one exception, all the plants of our previous expedition, and some others as well. Here the yew trees are bearing their curious male catkins; and their young green seeds, each terminating a twig, have a drop of sticky liquid at their apex to receive the pollen. We may find also upon them the artichoke-gall produced by the puncture of a special gnat. Here too the green hellebore, and the darker-hued evergreen stinking hellebore, with reddish blotches on its green sepals, are now bearing their little tubular petals filled with poisonous honey; and here in the recesses of some wood we may meet with the leathery bright green clustering leaves and the tough stalks of the spurge-laurel, the evergreen congener of the gay mezereon we saw in the farmhouse garden. Its greenish and inconspicuous tubular flowers have been open for some time, and may have lost both fragrance and honey; but its foliage is always attractive. Primroses may perhaps be absent; but their place is abundantly filled by the characteristic plant of the district, the true oxlip, or, as it is locally called, the "paigle." With leaves and peduncle much like those of the cowslip, and flowers not as broad as those of the primrose, it has a creamy tint of colour and an apricot-like perfume which are both peculiarly its own; and, unlike many rarities, in this district, where alone in the British Isles it does occur, it is abundant.

WILD LIFE:

FURRED AND FEATHERED.

———◆———

ALTHOUGH the rude winds of March may cause the
feebler wayfarers, whose blood runs slowly, to pu
plaid or cloak more closely about their sensitive frames,
they are propitious to the observer of life out of doors,
whether this be in the form of biped or quadruped. There
is a clearness of atmosphere which brings distant objects
nearer, and makes our observations more exact ; besides
which the great cloud masses get broken up and driven, in
all their varied tones of grey and pearly white, swiftly over
hill and dale, bringing about ever-varying effects of light
and shade. These keep a lover of nature in that pleasant
expectant attitude of mind that dispels all mental vapours,
and promotes a healthful light-hearted vigour of mind and
body which is eminently suited to the "going out for to
see" what may be stirring under the changeful skies.

Rough blasts cause hawks, jackdaws, and owls to seek a
shelter ; and this varies with different localities. In Surrey,
for instance, they find it to perfection in old workings that
have been abandoned, in the chalk hills where lime was
once burned ; cracks and rents in these lonely corners suit
the birds exactly. And the wild gusts cause the rooks to

gather thickly in the old trees, where they have been nesting from time immemorial. They assemble in great numbers to hold noisy confabulations about the mischief and damage that rude Boreas is likely to do amongst their nests, which are built so high up in the swaying branches. They croak and flap and caw in a great state of excitement. The new nests are constructed of green pliant twigs, which are laced into the forked and highest branches of the trees, so that the whole affair can swing freely to and fro as the wind blows. Now and again a fiercer gale than usual will blow some of them out of the trees bodily, but as a rule they can stand a great deal. It is too early to watch the birds in their busy domesticities; a little later on and father rook will have an active time of it, for he is a most attentive husband and parent; and not only does he provide amply, but he cackles pleasantly the while he feeds his mate, thus surely—to judge from humans and their ways in like case — making the morsels sweeter to the stay-at-home female bird.

Although, as I have said, windy March favours the general observer, yet this is not one of the best months for the bird lover, because it is the season when our winter visitors have either left or are thinking of leaving us. The woodcock, for instance, after having paired, will, the majority of them, take flight now, in order to nest in the vast forests of Scandinavia and Russia. Still, the numbers that remain with us are, owing to the great increase of plantations in large portions of our land—especially of the fir species—yearly becoming greater; but few of the spring migrants have as yet arrived. The exact time of the coming of these latter varies, of course, in different localities, as may be seen very clearly in the naturalist's calendar, which is appended to some editions of White's *Natural History of Selborne*, where the earliest and latest dates on which that ardent lover of nature in Hampshire noted their arrivals and departures, stand opposite to Markwick's notes of the same, as recorded near Battle, in Sussex. The weather, which often varies much in different localities, also influences the movements of birds greatly, and so the varied statements as to the comings and goings of migrants are easily accounted for.

About the slopes of the South Down hills myriads of small snails are now providing food for numbers of birds, appearing and vanishing according to the changes in the weather. These snails have remained in a torpid state during the winter, in holes of walls, under large stones, and in the ground, making their appearance only if the weather became very mild. Snails are said to have existed hidden away where no egress was possible, without food of any kind, for two and even three years. And speaking of snails, it is strange that they are not in more common use amongst us as an article of diet, since the Romans introduced the one called *helix pomatia* into our country, as a luxury of which they were fond. They are in great request in some parts of the Continent. When the mornings and evenings are moist and warm, the snails are everywhere, and worms show up also in great quantities that delight the plover.

The great plover, stone curlew, or thicknee, may be found on the downs and in the greater fields; his peculiar wild call note betrays his presence often, and you hear him "clamour" when you cannot catch a sight of him. The lonely shepherd on the Downs is not fond of his peculiar cry.

Lapwings or pewits are very active during the month of March, running hither and thither in search of suitable nesting places. Father pewit flaps his broad wings, sticks up his pretty crest, fusses about his mate, and together they peer into any little depression in the ground where bits of grass, twigs, and other unconsidered trifles have been blown. Or together with large companies of their kind they flap and wheel about in all directions over the upland pastures.

Crows are keenly looking out, for this is the time for them to pounce and feast on any unfortunate little lamb that may be disabled or helpless. The raven too has his mate to provide for just now, and woe betide any venturesome young rats that fall under his keen eyes. He is becoming rare excepting along our more rocky southern coasts, and in parts of the New Forest. Although he may be welcomed as a destroyer of rats, he is too fond of game, and, like the crow, of weakly ewes and lambs, to be welcome everywhere. His nest, if you are lucky enough to come on one of the old raven trees where the birds have nested year after year, you will find lined with deer's hair, rabbit's fur, and soft wool.

Not many of our birds nest in March; but the blackbirds are busy, in and out of the evergreens in our shrubberies, and in the country hedgerows, where they add egg to egg till they have four, five, or six. By the end of the month their broods will, many of them, be hatched out. The young of the early broods sometimes help the parents to feed the second brood of the season. With a noisy note of alarm, which the bird rattles out as you approach his nesting place, he flits from bush to bush, and with a characteristic habit of quickly raising his tail when he perches that makes him easily distinguished, even at dusk. In the South he is commoner than the thrush, but in the North I think the latter bird, which emulates the blackbird in the richness of his note, is the more often noted about the gardens. Both birds should be welcomed, on account of the slugs, snails, and insects, with their larvæ, that they devour. Later on they may steal some fruit, but "the labourer is worthy of his hire," and man is often only too selfish in his character of ruler over the beasts of the field and the fowls of the air.

Chack! chack! cries the wheatear as he flits along the hillocky pastures, having arrived early, to spend his summer with us. On open ground, on warrens, and the poorer land near the coast you will find him; and especially in numbers about our South Downs. Owing to that jerky white tail of his, he gets the name everywhere of "white-rump." A blue-grey back and rich rufous-coloured breast, dark wings, and broad, black tips to his white tail, make the wheatear a very noticeable bird. He is wary and shy to a degree, however, and next month at your approach he will flit uneasily from place to place, in order to divert your attention from the nest that will be so cautiously formed right up some old rabbit burrow, or hidden in a peat stack or the deep crevice of a stone wall. The eggs, of which you may see as many as seven in a nest, are of a very lovely pale blue, sometimes having tiny purple spots on them.

A Son of the Marshes says of the wheatear, "A timid creature and gentle, the shadow of a crow's wing thrown on the turf as the bird flies overhead, is enough to make him crouch and run for shelter. The shepherd and his lads know his weakness; and when he runs to hide from the cloud shadows that alarm him they cut a turf and form a little lean-to shelter, and set a horsehair noose, into which the bird runs." Great quantities of the wheatear are captured in this manner and sold for the table.

The lively stonechat stays with us throughout the year. A scolding little fellow he is, and he shows his dislike of the intruding stranger by uttering his note, h-weet, jur, jur! as he darts from one furze bush to another. A black head, white neck, and reddish breast and quick motions, make him a bright conspicuous object. "Little Jacky Blacky-topper" I have heard him called. A labourer on the roads just above Brighton was followed in his work along the ditches for many days during a hard frosty spell, by a pair of these birds. They picked up small trifles as he worked, and crumbs when he fed. And at last they became so tame that when the weather grew more than usually severe, the female bird would allow the man to put her in his pocket for a while, now and again, evidently enjoying the warmth. When it grew milder again the birds disappeared. The stonechat does not begin to build his nest till early in April.

If you hang a bone or two upon a garden tree, especially if your home chance to be not far from the woods, you may observe some of the tit species well. Close to the window of a cottage in Surrey, where I stayed last March, I used to delight in feeding these beautiful little birds. The great titmouse is a very handsome fellow, and one who makes himself easily at home; he will even frequent our gardens in the centre of London. Mr. Howard Saunders tells of an inverted flowerpot in the British Museum having contained three new nests. I know of an invalid lady who had a pole hung out from her bedroom window, at the end of which the half of a cocoa-nut shell was hung. In this a pair of tits nested, and she had great enjoyment in watching their pretty movements from the bed on which she lay. The great titmouse, the coal tit, the marsh tit, and the lovely little blue tit, all came to the tree where I hung my bone or bits of suet. The coal tit is not so often met with as the great tit and the blue tit, but you may happen to find his nest, lined with wool and moss and rabbit's fur, in an old mouse burrow in a bank—more often though in a hole of a tree stem or a crevice in a wall. Not till April, although that of the great tit is found earlier. The blue tit is called locally Billy-biter, owing to her plucky way of defending her young; she will peck at the fingers of the thief as she sits on her eggs, and hiss like a snake. These pretty little creatures ought to be encouraged in gardens, for they feed their young with the larvæ off our gooseberry bushes, and with aphides that infest the trees, whilst the parent birds devour the grubs of wood-boring beetles, maggots, spiders, and other insects. The marsh tit is supposed to be much less common than the two last mentioned, yet he may often be seen near rivers, about the alder trees and pollarded willows, and in orchards and gardens.

Another interesting bird to note, although more difficult to observe, is the tree creeper. It might almost be taken for some other creature instead of a bird, owing to the way it moves upwards, downwards, and round about the trunk of the old tree, on which it hunts for spiders and other insects that are to be found in the crevices of the bark. Its long curved claws help it in climbing, and the tail feathers being then depressed, the colouring of the bird too being brown and of a buff-white, it is not readily distinguishable from the lichen-marked tree trunk or branch. His shrill little song during this month may guide you to his whereabouts, but his nest will not be found till later on.

Tiniest of all our British birds is the bright little golden-crested wren, and these wrens arrive in great flocks on our east coast, of late years in increasing numbers, also owing to the larger cultivation of larches and fir trees. You may see them at such times like swarms of bees on bushes near the coast, and the weary little travellers on their migrating flight rest often in numbers about the rigging of fishing craft. During this month the male's little song is heard continually when the weather is fine; and he builds now his beautiful nest, of soft moss as a rule, underneath the branch of a yew, a cedar, fir, or perhaps one of your garden evergreens. It is cunningly felted with spider's webs, a little lichen, and soft wool, with a few tiny feathers. In this from five to ten mottled eggs will be laid. In the company of tits and creepers this bird may be seen looking for its insect food in the woods and spinneys.

The willow wren has arrived, and we hear a few faint little notes that seem to say he has not yet regained his strength and full song, being perhaps weary after his long flight to our shores. In April his voice will be stronger, and indeed he may not appear at all until early next month. A delicately-shaped greenish-yellow bird he is, the commonest of the warblers of his kind that visit us in the time of the vernal migration. Owing to the shape of his domed nest, which is made of dry grass lined with feathers, this bird, with the others of his species, is called the oven-bird, and to the willow wren is given also the name of hay-bird.

Its song consists only of a few reiterated notes, but soon it will take on quite a gay tone and make itself heard in every little grove.

Few birds are so beautifully marked, or rather we should say so delicately pencilled, as is the wryneck, the cuckoo's mate or herald, which comes to us always a few days in advance of the latter. "The merry pee bird" the song calls him. Pee-pee-pee he cries from the end of March right on till Midsummer. This is a bird that eludes observation; its short undulating flight makes it also difficult to observe. The name wryneck has been given to it owing to the peculiar way it has of twisting its neck round as it sits; it will hiss loudly too when disturbed on its nest, so that it is often called the snake bird. Country children hail its pee-pee-pee or pay-pay-pay, for the cuckoo is coming, they say, as they hear it; and somehow all children of smaller or larger growth are glad to note the first shoutings of the cuckoo. The wryneck's nest, with its pure white thin-shelled eggs, will be found generally in some hole in a tree-trunk, not far from the ground, and sometimes in a sandbank; but that will not be for nearly two months yet.

Now is the time to go and sit in some quiet nook of one of our Surrey woods, to listen for the yikeing laugh of the green woodpecker. Rain-bird he is called in some districts, because his loud pleu-pleu-pleu is supposed to tell that we may expect wet weather. Yaffle, too, is a name given to him, and a most startling effect his laughing-like notes have, falling, as they often do, on the still evening air. The yaffle makes a new hole for his nest each season, but he uses the old holes as a sleeping-place. The greater and lesser spotted woodpeckers too, you may hear; the latter is common enough not far from London; in the Thames valley for instance. From some old giant of the woods sounds this tap-tap-tap of the yaffingale, another name for the green woodpecker, as he works for his daily living on the tree-trunk, working his way up with short jerky movements in an oblique direction. His colouring of olive-green on the back, shading into yellow, with crimson crown and nape, attracts attention. His knowing-looking head appears for a moment round the trunk on which he is busy, on hearing the breaking of a dry twig beneath our feet; it startles and drives him with dipping flight to a more distant tree. Soon he will be hewing a neat round hole in a branch or bough of some softer wooded tree, and little chips of wood scattered about may guide you to one of these. His relative, the greater spotted woodpecker, is not so industrious; he will enlarge some natural cavity in an old decayed bough until it is of a size and shape that please him.

The nuthatch seeks for a suitable hole in the same fashion, in the branch of a tree or in some old wall. There it builds in much more scientific fashion than do the last-named birds, blocking up the entrance to its nest by skilful bird masonry, using as its materials for this purpose small stones and clay. A small opening is left for the birds' outgoings and incomings. The male utters a liquid flute-like note; during this month it is a shrill tui-tui-tui! Mr. F. Bond gave a nuthatch's nest to the British Museum, the weight of the clay used in the bird's work on this particular one being eleven pounds. It had been taken from a haystack; its measurements were thirteen inches by eight. The length of the bird itself is about five inches, and as it moves up and down a tree trunk with wonderfully quick motions, you might mistake its short, compact body for that of a mouse. The insects about the bark supply it with food, but in the autumn it enjoys hazel and beech-nuts. After picking one up among fallen leaves the little bird will carry it to a branch, where it rests it between the grooves of the bark, to hammer at it until the shell splits, and the kernel is laid bare.

The woodlark is not a very common bird, and it is most frequently found in our southern counties, such as Hampshire, Devon, and Dorset, also on the wooded sides of the Thames Valley. The tree pipit is mistaken by many for this bird. Its eggs will be laid by the middle of this month; they are of white or greenish-white, spotted and sometimes barred with a violet-grey and warm brown. The nest is firmly built of grass and some moss, lined with fine bents, and will be found in a depression of the ground, under some low bush, or now and again just in the smooth, open turf. The bird's song is sweet and liquid in its notes, and it is uttered pretty much throughout the year. You may be fortunate enough to watch the pretty performance of the woodlark, as it ascends from a branch on which it may have perched, singing as it mounts; it hovers in the air, suspended as it seems, and descends again, still singing, in a spiral direction, its wings half closed as though in the very ecstasy of its little song, on to the same branch from which it mounted.

The little chiff-chaff is the earliest of our spring visitors, and he utters his small song of chiff-cheff-cheef-chif! chevy-chevy-chevy! before the leaves are on the trees in sheltered willow holts, though he also frequents the branches of high trees, especially those of tall elms. He resembles his relative the willow wren, but may be distin-

D

guished from the latter by being smaller in size, and of duller tones of colouring, also by his more rounded wing. Male and female have the same plumage, the yellow tint being always brighter after the moulting season in the autumn. His nest is an oval, dome-shaped, the opening being rather to the top than the middle; it is composed of dry grass, leaves and moss, well lined with feathers. Sometimes this is placed in evergreens and other bushes, but usually amongst grasses and ferns, not far above the ground.

In the woods overhead the wood-pigeons or ring-doves are all alive, cooing, clapping their wings, spreading out their tails, and floating about. Their breeding season has begun; you may watch the birds coming and going to their slightly-built nests, which are composed of twigs laid crosswise in the larch-trees, or almost any kind of tree. Sometimes these are placed on the hollowed places where other birds have nested, or which squirrels have used. Grain of all sorts, peas, leaves, and bulbs of turnips form their diet, with beech-nuts and berries in their seasons. Farmers complain terribly of these voracious birds, but in writing of them a Son of the Marshes, whom it would be difficult for me to refrain from quoting, states that the Surrey farmer will grumble and say, "They comes to the fields, they gits in the corn, they gits all over the place, an' they spiles the turmits." I myself received a very well-written protest against these hungry birds from a young lady, the daughter of a large farmer on the higher lands above the Thames, fully endorsing the above-quoted complaints. Yet we learn further from the naturalist that two of the wild plants which are the farmers' worst foes are charlock and the wild mustard plant, and that the pigeons search out and feed on these as well as on other ill weeds, which is, as one may say, "a stone in the other pocket." Pigeons are very good to eat, and they may be a small source of revenue. Turtle-doves, which, however, are only summer visitors to our islands, and arrive some six weeks later on, are accused too of stealing (?) the farmers' oats ; but in point of fact they are extremely fond of a small vetch that grows plentifully at the roots of the oats. As a rule wild pigeons get their living in the woods and from the outskirts only of the fields.

The brown, tawny, or wood owls hoot in the woods, for this is their nesting season, and you may hear their uncanny cries during the daytime, although you will not easily distinguish the bird, as he will draw himself up closely to the tree-trunk, where he had perched on hearing the step of an intruder; and his tones of colouring, varied shades of ashen grey, mottled with brown, buffish white, and dark brown streaks, with large spots of white, harmonise so perfectly with the tones of the moss and lichen-covered bark, that the creature is to all intents and purposes invisible. He likes best to build in a hollow in some decayed old tree, pleasantly shadowed over by sprays of ivy. If you are wary and silent in your observations you may catch a glimpse of him as he settles on a shallow of some woodland stream, where he will enjoy a bath to the full, shaking the water out in all directions. The wood owl has the noble trait of constancy in his character, for he is said to mate for life, and the birds return each year to the same hole in the tree to nest. As soon as the first egg is laid they begin to sit, so that young and eggs are to be found together in one nest. Voles, rats, mice, moles, and shrews, form the greater part of their food, so they must be looked upon as great friends of the agriculturalist. Strange that ignorant superstition as to the habits and nature of this really fine bird should for so long have placed him under the ban of dislike and fear.

Unfortunately for that brilliantly-coloured bird the king-fisher, which lends such interest to the sides of our running brooks and streams—where the trout are now beginning to rise—as he flashes past with his shrill note of tit-tit-tit—a piping, rattle-like sound, his bright feathers have a good value in the market, where they are sold for the manufacture of artificial flies. So he is not abundant, in consequence, as he used to be, and the banks of lakes, ponds, and streams have lost many of these most picturesque fishers. Still the patient observer may, especially if he use a field-glass, note this bird as he sits perched with exemplary patience on a convenient bough projecting over the water, whence he darts with sudden plunge as soon as his keen eye has marked its prey. Upon a little layer of fish-bones his nest is to be found, or simply on the earth of some dry sandpit, or now and again in an old wall. Roundish glossy eggs will be laid there during this month—six, and even as many as ten of them sometimes. They have been hatched out frequently before the middle of the month. Besides taking small fishes, the kingfisher lives on crustaceans, dragon-flies, and water-beetles, of which he can stow away a marvellous quantity.

First of the swallow family to revisit our shores comes the cosy-looking little sand-martin, which we expect to-wards the end of March. He is the first of his tribe to come, and the first to leave us. A colony of sand-martins nesting in tunnels in the reddish-yellow sandstone of Surrey, is a pretty sight; they nest also in earth cliffs by the riverside, or in railway cuttings and gravel quarries, boring galleries which slant somewhat upwards, and making the nest in an enlarged space at the end of dry grass and plenty of feathers. Their eggs are pure white, four to six in number. Their song is only a faint twitter; gnats and other small insects compose their diet.

The ring-ousel is by no means a common bird, and he is the only bird of the thrush family that leaves us altogether during the winter. He may be with us at the end of this month, or may not appear until early in April. His comings and goings are irregular, and he is looked upon by the rustics in our Southern counties as a somewhat mysterious visitant. As a rule this bird prefers to haunt the banks of Northern streams, and the wild, hilly parts of Devon, Cornwall, the Welsh hills, and other high districts, where it feeds on the berries of the mountain-ash and the autumn moorland berries; worms, slugs, and insects satisfy it earlier, and what it can pick up in gardens near its haunts. Its motions are very different to those of the other thrushes, and these arrest the eye quickly, before one can distinguish the bird rightly. On the Surrey moors, which he visits at times only, sometimes singly, sometimes in flocks, where junipers abound, he feeds on those berries, but those of the mountain-ash he much prefers. On ledges of the rock or in the banks near the stream sides the ring-ousel—white-throated blackbird the country folks call him—likes to make his nest, although he has it also at times in the tall ling on the moors. Although you may see the bird this month, you will not find his nest so early.

*   *   *   *   *   *

In copses and spinneys the pheasant will be crowing and strutting about, with ear-tufts erect, puffed-out crimson cheek and burnished breast. He makes a brave picture, both as he steps along so daintily, and also as he shoots through the keen air of early spring, with his tail spread out, its central feathers swaying, fully deserving his name of rocketer—nearly four miles at one flight he has been known to take. The males are more than usually lively during the month of March, as they now put on their war paint in order to fight for the possession of the hen birds. They are useful in eating up a great quantity of wire worms, and other hurtful insects; later on they feed their young on ants and their larvæ. So do the partridges, which are now pairing. And as the black ants *(formica nigra)* appear first this month, I may be allowed to quote again from a Son of the Marshes an interesting statement as to these insects, as regards their furnishing food for the game birds just mentioned—

"Two very different kinds of ant hills supply the eggs or ant-pupæ to the young of game birds, and of partridges in particular. First, there are the common emmet heaps, or ant hills, which are scattered all over the land. These the birds scratch and break up, picking out the eggs as they fall from the light soil of the heaps, . . . But the ant eggs proper come from the nests or heaps of the great wood ants, either the black or the red ants."

The black appear in March, the red ones in April commonly. These heaps of the black ant are mounds of fir-needles, being in many instances as large at the bottom in circumference as a waggon-wheel, and from two to three feet in height—even larger where they are very old ones. They are found in fir woods, on the warm sunny slopes, under the trees as a rule, close to the stems of the trees. The partridges and their chicks do not visit these heaps, for they would get bitten to death by the ferocious creatures. The keepers and their lads procure their eggs ; a wood-pick, a sack, and a shovel are the implements used. Round the men's gaiters or trousers leather straps are tightly buckled to prevent, if possible, the great ants from fixing on them, as they will try to do, like bull-dogs, when the heaps are harried. The top of the heap is shovelled off, laying open the domestic arrangements of the ant heap, and showing also the alarmed and furious ants trying to carry off their large eggs to a place of safety; but it is all in vain—eggs and all, they go into the sack. In spite of every precaution the ant egg getters are bitten, often severely. The ants spit their strong acid out most venomously. You may know when a lot of heaps have been harried by the smell that greets your nostrils as you walk near, as though some coarse kind of aromatic vinegar had been poured out under the trees. Then too you may see thousands of the creatures raised up on their legs, their bodies bent under and forwards as they spray formic acid in all directions. If you are foolish enough to place your hand over the hollow in the heap you will not soon forget it.

*   *   *   *   *   *

The moorhen, or waterhen, disports himself now, in and out of the dead sedges, clucking and flirting up his pert-looking tail. He is thinking about nesting, and his mate will not be far from him. The cock moorhen has put on his breeding plumage, and although it is not a gaily-coloured one, it is rich in its tones if you can observe it closely. His legs are brightly coloured, a greenish yellow, having a red band above the tarsal joint, and he has a scarlet shield above the base of the bill. Together the pair will pick and poke about, clucking the while, until they have found a spot to their liking.

In our southern counties the mallards, or common wild ducks, will be hatching out their young. Their nests, made of grass and lined with down, are usually near fresh water, on the ground, but there is no rule as to this, for they may be found in hedgerows, in cornfields, and even in the forsaken nests of other birds up in the trees. Some have nested in the high trees near the Round Pond in Kensington Gardens; a very wise plan, as their eggs and young are safe there from thieving bipeds and quadrupeds. The fluffy little birds are soon able to take care of themselves, and the mallards do not trouble at all to provide for them. A friend of mine found one of their nests on the top of a hayrick, and they will also build in the farmer's faggot stacks.

And now is the time to watch for the fussy little grebe or dabchick, making arrangements for the family he intends to bring out from his damp nest. It is his time for amusing himself with his mate in and on the reedy stream or open pond, and it will nest on some of our waters in the London parks even. The dabchicks feed on small fish, insects, and vegetable matter. Their note is whit-whit. Later on the bird will be seen carrying its young on its back to and from the nest, that is moored to some aquatic plants.

Among the river tangle water-rails slip in and out, and the male seems to be bolder at this time than is his wont; for he shows himself openly as he walks along the edges of the reed-fringed pool, or runs here and there grunting and squeaking. Like the moorhens, he would be less noisy if he had his family with him; just now he has little to fear.

* * * * * *

And now a few words as to the reptiles we may possibly get a sight of in our wanderings this month. You may be —shall I say fortunate or unfortunate enough (?) to come across a viper—the common viper or adder, which is the only poisonous reptile of our country side. Its colour varies much, but if the creature you take for one has a row of zig-zag markings down the whole length of its back, there will be no mistake about its identity. About the centre of its head also you will note a clearly defined V-shaped dark mark. I know personally very many, not usually cowards, who love the country, yet whose walks are spoiled by a terror of straying into its most charming nooks lest they get bitten by a viper. Such an accident rarely happens; still it is as well, if you are in search of the wild white violet and the sweet primrose, to look round, if the spot you have chosen be a grassy bank, warmed by the sun that comes out on those days when blusterous March is going out meekly like the proverbial lamb. If you do not happen to touch the reptile with foot or hand as you stoop, he will never harm you. The viper is useful in its way, not because it still enables many a one to gain a little money by collecting what they call "adder-ile," but on account of its great proclivity for the young of mice, for which it hunts most assiduously—mice which, as many of them as are allowed to grow, would not only rob the bees of honey, but kill and eat up the bees themselves.

Coluber natrix, or the common grass snake, a perfectly harmless creature, will appear about the end of the month. Specimens from three to four feet in length are very common, sometimes they are as long as six feet when found in waste places near woods where gravel has been dug out. There, in and near little pools of water, the snake finds his food—small rabbits, mice, frogs, birds, and birds' eggs; that is, those of such as build on the ground among the brambles and wild tangle, satisfy him. You may see the creature glide in and out among the bushes and slender tree branches, or hanging head downwards from one apparently lifeless; till at your nearer approach the snake draws itself up in a moment, to shoot like a flash over and through the twigs. In colour this common snake is grey-green, lighter or darker, dotted over with black spots, having at the back of the head a yellow mark, bordered with black; it is yellow generally underneath, with black markings.

*   *   *   *   *   *

The frogs that were croaking last month are spawning now. If you take some of this spawn home with you and place it in water in a fish globe on your lawn, or in the town garden, it will give you much interest and amusement, as you watch its gradual development into little frogs. These will presently hop out all over your garden, where they will only do good. The snake leaves its coverts when the frogs spawn, and comes to the ditches to feed on them. The otter too will be glad to add them to his diet, so will stoats and weasels; as to the ducks, they had been raking out the frogs that had lain buried under the mud all the winter, and filling themselves with frog for some time past.

Then there is our common toad, now busy destroying great quantities of insect life; the bee-keeper dreads his proximity to the hives and kills him without remorse. Yet he is a good friend to the gardener, and he will remain long in some shady corner, doing only good by his presence. In melon and cucumber frames, and where grapes are grown, he is very useful. The natterjack toad differs from his more common relative by having a bright buff line down the middle of his back, and his movements are quicker than those of the first-mentioned.

*   *   *   *   *   *

The hare is liveliest in the month of March. The proverb that maligns by calling him mad at once recurs to the mind. His antics and gestures have caused him also to be styled "the merry-hearted brown hare." The fox and the stoat seek after his life, but puss is generally a match for these. Many other foes too he has, and of these man is the chief. He has his seat on the borders of woods, as well as on the hillside. Again on the wild marshlands he grows to a large size, and is very numerous. Nor is he actually timid, as another proverb asserts; and as he can swim and jump with such agility, not to mention his feats in boxing, we must certainly give him credit for some accomplishments.

The wild rabbits are busy with their young, and in many a coppice you will see the gamekeeper's lads about with the ferrets. The female rabbits go to the ploughed fields often now to make their stops, where they rear their young in less fear than if they stayed about the warrens, where the males are apt to harass, and foes take tithe of the small bunnies.

All these things, and much more of which we have not space to tell, we may observe in March—

> ". . . whose kindly days, and dry,
> Make April ready for the throstle's song."

Or, as Leigh Hunt said, in the beautiful chorus of the flowers, "the March winds pipe to make our passage clear."

APPENDIX.

PLANTS MENTIONED UNDER MARCH.

Aconite, Winter . . .	*Eranthis hyemalis.*
Alder	*Alnus glutinosa.*
Anemone	*Anemone hortensis.*
Anemone, Wood . .	*A. nemorosa.*
Apple	*Pyrus Malus.*
Aspen	*Populus tremula.*
Beans	*Faba vulgaris.*
Blackthorn	*Prunus spinosa.*
Box	*Buxus sempervirens.*
Briar	*Rosa canina.*
Brussels Sprouts . .	*Brassica oleracea gemmifera.*
Buckthorn	*Rhamnus catharticus.*
Butcher's Broom . .	*Ruscus aculeatus.*
Celandine, Lesser . .	*Ranunculus Ficaria.*
Celery	*Apium graveolens.*
Chickweed	*Stellaria media.*
Coltsfoot	*Tussilago Farfara.*
Cowslip	*Primula veris.*
Cow-parsley . . .	*Anthriscus sylvestris.*
Crocus	*Crocus vernus, versicolor,* &c.
Crown Imperial . .	*Fritillaria imperialis.*
Cuckoo Pint . . .	*Arum maculatum.*
Currant, Red . . .	*Ribes rubrum.*

Daisy	*Bellis perennis.*
Daffodil	*Narcissus Pseudo-narcissus.*
Dandelion . . .	*Taraxacum officinale.*
Dead Nettle, Red . . .	*Lamium purpureum.*
Dog's Mercury . . .	*Mercurialis perennis.*
Elm, Wych . . .	*Ulmus montana.*
Elder	*Sambucus nigra.*
Furze, Common . . .	*Ulex europæus.*
Furze, Dwarf . . .	*U. nanus & U. Gallii.*
Gooseberry . . .	*Ribes Grossularia.*
Ground Ivy . . .	*Nepeta Glechoma.*
Groundsel . . .	*Senecio vulgaris.*
Guelder Rose . . .	*Viburnum.*
Hazel	*Corylus Avellana.*
Hellebore, Green . . .	*Helleborus viridis.*
Hellebore, Stinking . .	*H. fœtidus.*
Hutchinsia, Rock . . .	*Hutchinsia petræa.*
Hyacinth, Cluster . . .	*Muscari racemosum.*
Hyacinth, Grape . . .	*M. botryoides.*
Hyacinth, Starch . . .	*Muscari.*
Hyacinth, Wild . .	*Scilla nutans.*
Larch	*Larix europæa.*
Marsh Marigold . . .	*Caltha palustris.*
Mezereon . . .	*Daphne mezereum.*
Mistletoe . . .	*Viscum album.*
Moschatel . . .	*Adoxa Moschatellina.*
Oxlip . . .	*Primula elatior.*
Oats . . .	*Avena sativa.*
Orchis, Early Purple . .	*Orchis mascula.*
Peas, Field . . .	*Pisum arvense.*
Poplar, White . . .	*Populus alba.*
Poplar, Hoary . . .	*P. canescens.*
Primrose . . .	*Primula vulgaris.*
Quick	*Cratægus Oxyacantha.*
Ribes	*Ribes sanguineum.*

Sallow	*Salix cinerea.*
Sallow, Great . . .	*S. Caprea.*
Saxifrage, Three-fingered . .	*Saxifraga tridactylites.*
Saxifrage, Golden . . .	{ *Chrysosplenium alternifolium* & *C. oppositifolium.*
Scorpion Grass, Early . .	*Myosotis collina.*
Scorpion Grass, Field . .	*M. arvensis.*
Shepherd's Purse . . .	*Capsella Bursa-pastoris.*
Snowdrop	*Galanthus nivalis.*
Speedwell, Ivy-leaved . .	*Veronica hederæfolia.*
Spurge Laurel . . .	*Daphne Laureola.*
Spurge, Wood . . .	*Euphorbia amygdaloides.*
Strawberry, Barren . .	*Potentilla Fragariastrum.*
Trifolium	*Trifolium incarnatum.*
Tulip	*Tulipa Gesneriana.*
Violet	*Viola odorata.*
Violet, Hairy . . .	*V. hirta.*
Violet, Wood . . .	*V. sylvatica.*
Wheat	*Triticum vulgare.*
Whitlow Grass, Spring . .	*Erophila vulgaris.*
Whitlow Grass, Yellow Alpine .	*Draba aizoides.*
Willow, Dwarf . . .	*Salix repens.*
Willow, Purple . . .	*Salix purpurea.*
Yellow Star of Bethlehem .	*Gagea fascicularis.*
Yew	*Taxus baccata.*